The CR
TRICK or TREAT

PURPLE

BLACK

HarperCollins *Children's Books*

DREW DAYWALT   OLIVER JEFFERS

The crayons are ready
for Halloween.

They can't wait to fill
their bags with treats.

Waltham Forest Libraries S

Please return this item by the last date stamped. The loan may be renewed unless required by another customer.

4/10/22		

Need to renew your books?
http://www.walthamforest.gov.uk/libraries or
Dial 0333 370 4700 for Callpoint – our 24/7 automated telephone renewal line. You will need your library card number and your PIN. If you do not know your PIN, contact your local library.

First published in the USA by Philomel Books,
an imprint of Penguin Random House LLC, i
First published in the United Kingdom by
HarperCollins *Children's Books* in 2022

HarperCollins *Children's Books* is a division
of HarperCollins*Publishers* Ltd
1 London Bridge Street, London SE1 9GF

www.harpercollins.co.uk

HarperCollins*Publishers*
1st Floor, Watermarque Building,
Ringsend Road, Dublin 4, Ireland

10 9 8 7 6 5 4 3 2 1

Text copyright © Drew Daywalt 2022
Illustrations copyright © Oliver Jeffers 2022
Design by Rory Jeffers

Published by arrangement with Philomel, an imprint
of Random House LLC

ISBN: 978-0-00-856074-4

Printed in Latvia

You know what you're supposed to say at Halloween, Right?

OF COURSE WE DO.

Orange knocks
on the first door.

GIVE US
YOUR Treats, lady.

I'm Naked!

WHAT???

OK. That was
ALL KINDS OF WRONG.

NOT TO MENTION
CONFUSING!

Green knocks on
the next door.

Ok, it's HALLOWEEN!
And we have to be polite too.

Oh, POLITE!
OK we get it now.

Grey knocks on
the door after that.

Oh for crying
out loud!

Points For good manners,
I guess.

It's a <u>SCARY</u> DAY, Everyone!

OH SCARY. OK, I've got this one!

White knocks
on the door.

BOO!

Feeeeeeek!

That's not quite
what I meant...

It WAS close, though.

Grey steps
forward again.

WAIT!

Repeat after me:
Trick. Or. Treat.

There we go.

The crayons all
knock on the door.

TRICK OR

And also... **BOO!**